LADYBIRD BOOKS, INC.
Auburn, Maine 04210 U.S.A.
© LADYBIRD BOOKS LTD 1989
Loughborough, Leicestershire, England

Printed in U.S.A.

Where Is Grandma Rabbit?

By Stephanie Calmenson
Illustrated by Carolyn Bracken

Ladybird Books

Grandma Rabbit was fast asleep in her warm, cozy bed when...

Ring-a-ling-a-ling! The telephone rang.

"Hello," said Grandma, sleepily.

"Hello, Grandma!" said Sam, wide awake. "Are you ready to take us to Playland?"

"Playland? Oh, dear," said Grandma Rabbit. "I was out dancing until late last night. And now I am so sleepy."

"But, Grandma! You promised!" said Tilly, Sam's twin sister.

Grandma Rabbit swung her feet over the side of the bed. "Grandma Rabbit keeps her promises!" she said. "I'll be there in a jiffy."

Grandma Rabbit got dressed, hopped onto her bicycle, and hurried over to Sam and Tilly's house.

"Hooray for Grandma Rabbit!" said Sam and Tilly when she arrived.

They got to Playland in no time at all.

"Which ride would you like to go on first?" asked Grandma. "How about a nice, slow ride on the Ferris wheel?"

"Oh, no!" said Sam. "We want to go on the roller coaster!"

So Grandma Rabbit bought three tickets for the roller coaster.

The cars chugged up to the top of the tracks.

"Gosh!" said Tilly. "Look how high up we are!"

Before they knew it, the roller coaster had picked up speed and was whizzing down the other side of the tracks.

"Wheeee!" cried Grandma Rabbit. "This is fun!"

"What's next?" asked Grandma, getting into the spirit. "Shall we try the Big Snake or the Moon Rocket?"

"Let's find Captain Bigwig's Air Show," said Sam. "Everyone at school is talking about it."

"Come on, then," said Grandma Rabbit.

At the Air Show, Grandma flew higher than anyone else. Captain Bigwig himself was waiting to greet them when they got off. "You're quite a pilot," he said to Grandma Rabbit.

"Why, thank you," she said, blushing just a little.

"Wow, Grandma!" said Sam, as they walked away. "Captain Bigwig talked to you!"

"Wait till we tell them at school," said Tilly.

They decided to try the parachute jump next.

"Look out below!" called Grandma on the way down.

When they were back on the ground, Grandma said,
"I'm feeling a little tired. I think it's time for
a slow ride now."

"There's one," said Sam. He pointed to a sign
that said HARRY'S HAUNTED HOUSE.

"Well, at least we'll be sitting down," said
Grandma Rabbit as she bought the tickets.

Tilly and Sam got into one boat. Grandma got into another. And they all sailed off into a deep, dark tunnel.

"It's spooky in here," said Sam.

"Look out!" cried Tilly. "There's a ghost!"

Tilly and Sam covered their eyes.

As soon as the boat stopped, Tilly and Sam hurried onto the dock.

"That was really scary," said Sam.

"Oh, I wasn't so scared," said Tilly. "Were you scared, Grandma?" She turned to look at Grandma, but Grandma wasn't there.

"Uh-oh!" said Tilly. "Where is Grandma Rabbit?"

"We'd better go to the Lost and Found," said Sam.
"That's where you go when you lose something."

But no one at the Lost and Found had seen Grandma Rabbit.
So Tilly and Sam waited...and waited...and waited.

While they waited they worried.

"How could we leave her in that Haunted House?"
moaned Tilly.

"What if she was kidnapped by goblins?" cried Sam.

Sam and Tilly were wondering what to do next when they heard someone say, "Excuse me, can anyone here help me? I have lost my goggles."

It was Captain Bigwig!

Tilly raced over to him. "Your goggles are on your head," she whispered.

Captain Bigwig reached up. "So they are!" he said. "Thank you very much." Then he took a closer look at Sam and Tilly. "Weren't you on my ride this morning with your lovely grandmother?" he asked.

"Yes," said Sam. "But we've lost Grandma Rabbit!"

Now it was Captain Bigwig's turn to help. "Have no fear," he said. "I think I know how to find her!"

And he hurried off.

Meanwhile, back at the Haunted House, Grandma Rabbit was just waking up.

"My, my," she yawned. "I must have dozed off. I'd better find Tilly and Sam."

When she got outside, she saw a crowd gazing up at the sky.

"What's going on?" she asked a nearby goat.

"Captain Bigwig is writing a message in the sky," he replied.

Grandma Rabbit looked up and saw:

GRANDMA RABBIT COME TO THE LOST AND FOUND

"That's me!" said Grandma, and she began to run.

GRANDMA RABBIT COME TO THE LOST AND FOUND

"Grandma!" shouted Tilly and Sam. "Where were you?"

"I fell asleep in the boat," said Grandma.

Just then, Captain Bigwig returned. "Ah, Grandma Rabbit," he said. "I am so glad we found you. To celebrate your happy return, will you come dancing with me tonight?"

"I would love to!" said Grandma Rabbit.

"May we come too, Grandma?" asked Tilly and Sam.

"Absolutely not," said Grandma. Then she added, "But I promise to tell you all about it."

So together they danced all the way home...

…and Grandma and Captain Bigwig danced late into the night.

TheEnd

theEND